THE BIGGEST SPLASH

For Bob Case, my grandad

OXFORD
UNIVERSITY PRESS

Great Clarendon Street, Oxford OX2 6DP

Oxford University Press is a department of the University of Oxford.
It furthers the University's objective of excellence in research, scholarship,
and education by publishing worldwide in

Oxford   New York

Auckland   Cape Town   Dar es Salaam   Hong Kong   Karachi
Kuala Lumpur   Madrid   Melbourne   Mexico City   Nairobi
New Delhi   Shanghai   Taipei   Toronto

With offices in

Argentina   Austria   Brazil   Chile   Czech Republic   France   Greece
Guatemala   Hungary   Italy   Japan   Poland   Portugal   Singapore
South Korea   Switzerland   Thailand   Turkey   Ukraine   Vietnam

Oxford is a registered trade mark of Oxford University Press
in the UK and in certain other countries

Database right Oxford University Press (maker)

First published 2005

British Library Cataloguing in Publication Data available

ISBN: 978-0-19-272570-7

10 9 8 7 6 5 4

Printed in China

Paper used in the production of this book is a natural, recyclable product
made from wood grown in sustainable forests. The manufacturing process
conforms to the environmental regulations of the country of origin.

THE BIGGEST SPLASH

Thomas Taylor

OXFORD
UNIVERSITY PRESS

One hot day, Clovis was sitting by
the lake doing nothing naughty at all.
Suddenly, he noticed something strange.

Another tiger was looking up
at him from under the water.

This was
worrying.

'Tigers can't swim!' cried Clovis.
'They NEVER go in the water!'

He ran to find something to
help the other tiger get out.

He spotted
a long vine.

TWANG!

He pulled it free and
ran back to the lake.

'Grab hold of this!' shouted Clovis.
But the underwater tiger just
stared at him.

So Clovis ran to
the old tree trunk.

RUMBLE!

He rolled it
down
to the lake.

SPLASH!

'Hold on to this!'
shouted Clovis.
But the underwater tiger
just waved his paws.

'Maybe one of my friends
can help,' said Clovis.
'Someone who can swim.
Because tigers NEVER
go in the water.'

His friend, Hortense, was enjoying a peaceful wallow when — **sploosh sploosh sploosh** — there was Clovis.

'Help!' he said. 'There's a tiger trapped under the water. And tigers can't swim!'
'Now, Clovis,' said Hortense. 'I'm sure there isn't really a tiger under the water.'

Sploosh!

'There is!' shouted Clovis. 'Look!'

Hortense stuck her head under the water.
'No tigers down here,'
she bubbled.

Clovis leant over.
   'But there is a tiger,' he said.
            'A really frightened one!'

'Now, Clovis,' said Hortense. 'Don't get upset.
Why don't you jump in and rescue him yourself?'

'Me?'
said Clovis.
'But tigers can't swim!'

'Brave tigers can,'
said Hortense.

Clovis knew what
he had to do.

He took a deep breath,
closed his eyes, and…

SPLOOOSH!

It was the
biggest
splash
he had ever made.

Down,

down,

down,

went Clovis, right to the bottom of the water.
He opened his eyes.
There was **no** underwater tiger to be seen.

Clovis bobbed back up.
'I'm floating!' he said.
'But where's the
underwater tiger?'

'Clovis, it was you,'
said Hortense.
'Me?'

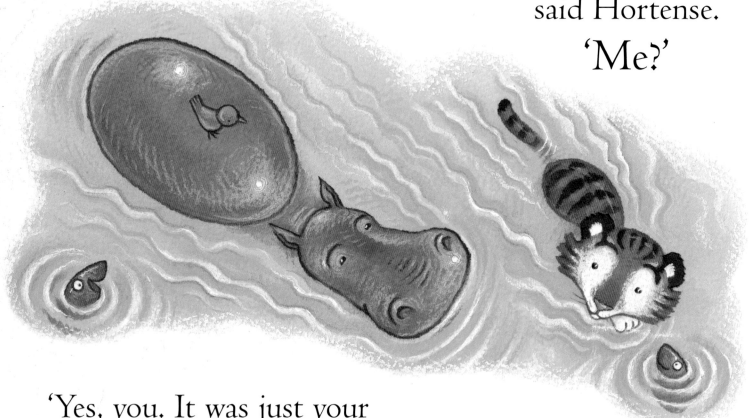

'Yes, you. It was just your
reflection,' Hortense explained kindly.
'Now kick your legs and you'll be able to swim.'

Clovis kicked.
'I'm swimming!' he shouted.
'I can do it.
Tigers love swimming!'

And everyone loved swimming with Clovis . . .

SF/2008034